I0726609

I WILL TEACH YOU RETRIBUTION

I Will Teach You Retribution

Stories

Timothy Moore

Long Day Press
Chicago

Copyright © 2023 Timothy Moore
Published by Long Day Press
Chicago, Il 60647
LongDayPress.com
@LongDayPress

ISBN 978-1-950987-37-5 (Paperback Edition)
ISBN 978-1-950987-39-9 (eBook Edition)
Library of Congress Control Number: 2023943076

Edited by Joseph Demes
Cover and Layout by Joshua Bohnsack

Printed in the United States of America.
First Edition

Contents

The horrors had moved outside Horace's apartment. Not even policemen and their ladies are safe, the horrors thought. No one is safe. Safety does not exist. Ha ha ha ha ha ha ha ha ha!

—Donald Barthelme

MY HUSBAND'S
RIGHT HAND IS
RIDDLED WITH
GLASS AND
HE'S SCREAMING,

MY HUSBAND
RIDDLED WITH
GLASS MY HUSBAND'S
MY SCREAMING WITH
GLASS. AND
RIGHT RIDDLED WITH SCREAMIN
RIDDLED GLASS AND HUSBA
WITH SCREAMING,
HE'S GLASSY AND HUSBAND HAND'S
MY SCREAMING WITH
RIGHT HAND'S
RIGHT HAND'S GLASS AND HUSBA
RIDDLED WITH HUSBAND
HE'S SCREAMIN
RIDDLED GLASS RIGHT HAND'S
GLASS SCREAMING,
RIDDLED WITH

the glass so deep that it's jammed in the bone, and when he pulls out the shards it's like plucking petals from an angry tulip. I am the cause of his glass hand. I crushed the glass to shards and filled a jar with sand. I made sure there was more sand than glass. I told him in the jar there was a prize, my shining love, and if he reached deep enough he would find it.

His hand is shimmering below the sun. I once thought his hands were the fairest. Now, his right is sharp and terrible. Don't pick up the baby with that! He thinks he can judge me, says that I am an unfit mother. That I will someday endanger us all. But he is the one who sticks his hand in unmarked jars. He will know the truth later.

My original plan: A bathtub full of glass. My man should be so lucky: to be dressed entirely in glass, marched down the street as the Living Mirror Man. Children would stare into his Eternity, and in their eyes my husband would discover himself. He is not so lucky, after all. One hand is all that will be adorned.

His hand is my mirror. His hand is my face. He plucks the petals, glares at me. He found my love and is no longer wanting.

ASS; OR

WHAT'S EATING BILL

ASS, OR
WHAT'S EATIN

WHAT'S EATIN BILL
OR

HAT'S BILL ASS; O
EATING

BIL WHAT'S EATIN
O

WHAT'S EATIN

ASS, OR
WHAT'S EATIN BILL

WHAT'S EATIN
HAT'S EATIN BILL

Before they saw it, Bill, Jake, and Mike were digging so a pipe could be inserted into the ground, in the city, on the hottest day of the year, the three of them weighed down by their tools and hard yellow hats, and of the three Bill was the one who saw it first, scratched his whiskers, brushed his bald head and said to Mike, "Will you look at that ass," and Mike saw it, stretching at the jeans, round and voluptuous, and said, "Damn, hot damn," and whistled, and called out to the ass, saying, "Hey, why don't you come back and I'll show you what I can do with that," and humped the air and whistled and nudged Jake, who didn't seem into the ass at all, which Mike was the first to notice and say, to make him notice the ass, "Look at that ass," and Jake looked, but then looked again because the ass had stopped, had turned, and they saw where the ass was coming from: a man: a thin man, sure, a fit man, a young man, even maybe a pretty man, but a man and so: a man's ass, and when the ass's man stared at the three men digging their hole for the pipe, the man's face was of complete astonishment, and he and his ass turned away from them, unaware of the damage that he had done with the ass that he had wrought.

"Didn't know I was working with a couple of gays," Jake said.

"No," Mike said. "No," he said again.

"Fuck off, the both of you," Bill said, and he dug deeper into the hole, never looking up, penetrating the Earth with his shovel.

"Do you want me to get his number?"

"No," was all Mike could say. He was looking at the sky, thinking hard. "Shit," he finally said.

"Funniest thing," Jake said, "the other guys are going to get a kick out of this."

"Don't you dare," Mike said. "If you say anything I will kill you."

Jake looked at him. "Go on and kill me then," he said.

At lunch, Jake didn't say anything to the rest of the guys, but he smiled at Bill and Mike, Mike who was prepared to pounce on Jake in front of everyone and bloody his face since he was no longer that scrawny little kid who was called Gay! Gay! Gay! all throughout middle school because his mother moussed his hair and made him wear a pink shirt one unfortunate Easter, since which he had amassed tremendous strength from twenty years of digging, the strength of a man — which he was now: a man — and a man would not tolerate having his manhood questioned, would not tolerate being suspect, no; a man would, in fact, pounce on Jake if he said anything to the other men, then throw him into the hole they just dug, then stick a pipe up his ass. Then he thought, "Fuck." Because that made him think about the ass.

Bill wouldn't say anything. He just ate his sandwich. He was worried that anything he said would provoke Jake to tell the rest of the guys what Mike and he had done, and what would he do then: Deny? Admit? And if the latter, what would that make him? Worse, what would that make him in the eyes of the other men? Better not to say anything. Like he wasn't even there.

One of the other guys noticed he was being aloof and said, "What's eating Bill?" And Jake wanted to say, "Ass," but he didn't.

When Mike arrived home the game was already on the TV. His wife asked him if he'd picked up the eggs like she'd asked, and he told her to shut the fuck up. He then picked her up, slapped her ass and fucked her on the living room floor, while Aaron Jones ran in touchdown after touchdown, flawlessly. When Bill arrived home, he immediately began making dinner because his wife worked late. He peeked his head into the living room, right at that first touchdown when Mike began fucking his wife, then looked at his watch, then found a Victoria's Secret catalogue on the kitchen counter. He masturbated right there, in the kitchen, next to the frying pan. But it took him a long time. Jake sat and watched the game on a small TV from his deck outside. He smoked a cigar and puffed it in his wife's face. Jake was younger than Bill and Mike, but looked older than both of them and had been in marketing for a while before he started digging for pipes, so he had not amassed anything close to Mike's man-strength. Most nights he was left wholly depleted. Some nights he felt like he could barely move. His wife was a cute little button and she coughed when he blew smoke at her and she giggled and said, "Asshole." And then when she said that it reminded him of that perfect, scrumptious ass, and he said, "That reminds me," and he told her how Mike and Bill had been hooting and hollering when they saw an ass.

"You're not doing that, are you?" she said, and he said, "That's not the point," and told her about the ass and whence the ass came — this young pretty man, man purse, small leather jacket, but totally a man — and how they were looking at his ass, wanted to fuck his ass, how perfect it all was, and he started laughing so hard that he felt tears on his cheeks, but she wasn't laughing, not at all.

"I don't get it," she said. "What's so funny about that?" Alarm was creeping into her eyes. Whenever she looked at him like that it felt like she was onto something about him that he himself did not have the ability to see, or the language to articulate.

"It's not funny if I have to explain it," he said, and blew smoke in her face again.

The next day, Jake didn't say anything about the ass and that made Mike worry even more, because it was like he was holding that ass over him, just leering with the ass over him, so the first pretty girl he saw — and he made sure this time it was a girl — he dropped his shovel and ran up to her (couldn't have been more than twenty, freckles, tote bag, arms around her breasts, hiding her breasts), and said, "Hey, beautiful," and took his helmet off, and said, "you just made my day, with just your beautiful face, you're so beautiful," which Bill heard and which made Bill look at Jake and say, "What the fuck?" which made Jake smile and say, "He's trying."

That week, Mike, who had never cheated on his wife before, cajoled three phone numbers, and on his day off met one of the girls whose number he'd cajoled, who he couldn't bring home with him and who had roommates that were at her place, who he convinced to have sex with him in one of the storage trailers at work, and who was caught having sex with Mike by Bill, who shook his head, turning away from the both of them and saying, "Jesus, man, what the fuck are you doing?" And all Mike could do was smile, bare-assed, sweating proudly, like he'd made his point.

Bill took the Victoria's Secret magazine everywhere he went, and every time that ass would get in his head he would pull it out and look through the pages, read the breasts, which one time he had to do on the subway even, on the way home from work, and an old lady had sat next to him and said, "Do you mind?" in that way old ladies do, pointing at the magazine, the filth, and he'd turned to her, and feeling a little like Mike, could only smile and say, "Hey, I can't help myself," and a part of him hated himself for that but that self-hate felt right and true, like it was what being a real man was all about.

And still Jake said nothing. Bill eyed him suspiciously. Mike ignored the both of them and had become completely anti-social, quick to anger and despair. They no longer joked or talked sports; they stuck to their jobs. Their coworkers found their cold efficiency unnerving and began avoiding them at lunch and never invited them out after work. It was strange and fitting that their very disdain for each other had left them isolated from anyone else. Eventually Devon, the site manager, noticed, and said they would have to slow down or they'd get done too quickly and then there would be no more of "This," and he rubbed his thumb to his fingers. He laughed and his three gold teeth shined.

Bill found himself masturbating so much to Victoria's Secret magazines that he no longer had the energy or desire to have sex with his wife when she came home. One night, she rolled next to him in bed, in a frenzy. "Jesus, Bill," she said, "Come on, throw me a fucking bone here," and she took off her panties and she began rubbing herself on him and he saw her ass and he saw that ass and he couldn't fuck her, even though he was hard as a rock, he wouldn't fuck her. He knew that it would change everything he knew about himself to fuck her while thinking about that ass. "Why are you punishing me?" she said. And the look he gave scared her.

The next day, when they were finally about to insert

the lines of pipe in the ground, Jake broke down and said to Bill and Mike, "Why don't we do this?" and his left eye had a slight twitch when he said that and had been twitching on and off for a month. His wife, who used to drop off donuts and coffee once a week had not been seen in some time, and if anyone had cared enough about Jake to ask about her he would have told them that the bitch was visiting her sister and had given no indication of when she would grace him with her return. "You both tell me why you loved that guy's ass," Jake said. "And I won't tell anyone. I'll never bring it up again." He smiled, but there was no humor behind his teeth. In fact, there was something evil behind that smile of Jake's, as if by agreeing to this proposition, Bill and Mike would be sealing a pact with the devil himself and forfeiting their very souls.

Bill heard himself saying to Jake, "No. No more games. Go ahead. Tell everyone what we did. I don't care anymore." He looked to Mike for support, but the man was seething, his hands clenched white. Jake didn't even bother to challenge him, he just shook his head like Bill was ruining all of the fun. His sudden passivity gave Bill a second wind. He was onto something.

"Who cares if we liked that ass? Who cares where it came from?" He looked at Mike. Was he crying?

"None of this bullshit matters," he said to him. "It's just an ass." Mike seemed taken aback by what Bill had said. "Just an ass?" he said quietly. Bill felt himself shoved to the ground and he thought Jake had pushed him. But to his surprise, and terror, he saw that it was Mike, whose hands twisted around Bill's neck, pressing firmly into his windpipe; Mike, whose words were the last Bill heard before he blinked in and out until he was gone; Mike, who screamed, "Perfection matters!"

GIANT EATS, HAS EXISTENTIAL CRISIS

GIANT EATS
HAS EXISTENTI
AS EXISTENTIAL
CRISIS GIANT IS EAT
CRISIS GIANT EAT EA
GIANT HAS EXISTENTIA
TIAN EATS
HAS EXISTENT EXISTENTI
CRISIS
AS EXISTENTIAL EAT
CRISIS GIANT
GIANT EATS
HAS GIANT EXISTENT EA
HAS EXISTENTIAL
AN CRISIS EXISTENT
CRISIS GIANT EAT
EXISTENTIAL CRISIS

Giant Eats

I SO HUNGRY! LIKE DYING I SO HUNGRY! AND THEN I SEE HUMAN MILKING COW. I GOBBLE MILK FROM BUCKET. MILK GROSS. THEN I EAT COW. COW ALSO GROSS. NOT SURE WHY I THOUGHT WOULD NOT BE. THEN I BITE HUMAN. HE SAY, "don't eat me" AND I SAY, "TOO LATE" AND THEN I EAT HIM! I BITE HIS HEAD AND THEN SHOULDER AND CHEST AND PENIS AND THEN I JUST SWALLOW THE REST! THEN I FALL SLEEP ON HOUSE. HOUSE MADE OF STRAW AND WOOD. HOUSE HURT BACK BUT STILL, I SLEEP.

Giant Eats Again

I STILL SO HUNGRY! I FIND SCHOOL AND CHILDREN OUTSIDE PLAY. CHILDREN SCREAM! I SAY, "I DO NOT EAT YOU CHILDREN!" I DON'T EAT CHILDREN BECAUSE I MORE OR LESS GOOD BUT STILL THEY RUN AWAY AND MAKE ME SAD. AND THEN EVERYTHING GO RED SO I SLAP HANDS ON GROUND AND THEY FALL AND I KICK SCHOOL AND THEN I GRAB FIVE CHILDREN AT A TIME AND I CAN'T CONTROL ME I THROW THEM IN MOUTH AND I DO EAT THEM, THEY JUST KID BUT I SWALLOW THEM WHOLE! THEY SCREAM DOWN MY THROAT! IT ECHO AND TICKLE UNTIL THEY STOP AND THERE IS QUIET. THEN SCHOOL TEACHER SAY, _{"how could you eat them?"} AND I SAY, "THEY MEAN AND TASTE LIKE SUGAR LIKE CANDY" AND SHE SAY, _{"you monster"} AND I SAY, "YOU DESSERT" AND THEN I EAT HER FEET AND SHE SCREAM AND I EAT HER LEG AND VAGINA AND STOMACH AND SHE

TASTE LIKE SAD SALTY CRY AND I BURP HER FOR HOUR UNTIL I FIND RIVERBED AND I SLEEP ON RIVERBED.

Giant Has
Existential Crisis

WHEN I WAKE I NOT THAT HUNGRY BUT SAD FOR EATING CHILDREN. I NAKED SO I COLD TOO. SCHOOL TEACHER RIGHT. NO ONE LOVE ME. I ALONE ALWAYS. WHY I EXIST? NO GIANT EXCEPT ME. I DON'T REMEMBER EVEN FAMILY. LIKE I BORN FROM SKY OR FROM GROUND. I CRY. I FIND FAMILY OF DUCK IN RIVERBED. WHEN I SAD I EAT TO SATE PAIN. I EAT ALL DUCKS BARELY REGISTER AS FOOD SO SMALL QUACK QUACK. I SCRATCH SKIN AND EAT SKIN FLAKE. I EAT ME SO I KNOW ME AND SO I KNOW I TASTE TOO. I TASTE LIKE SAND AND ROT. I WISH SOMEONE EAT ME BESIDES ME. DARK SO I FIND VALLEY AND I SLEEP AND WANT SLEEP FOREVER.

Giant Rages Against
His Continued Existence

SILVER KNIGHT WAKES ME. HE HAS SWORD AND HELMET AND FLAG. HE SCREAM, _{"you will pay for eating children,"} AND I SAY, "YOU RIGHT! SLAY ME!" AND HE TRY TO SLAY ME HE CUT LEG AND POKE AT TESTICLES. TICKLES. HE STAB MY TOE AND I FEEL TICKLE. I DON'T WANT TICKLE I WANT HURT SO I SCREAM, "WILL YOU SLAY ME!" AND HE SAY, _{"'i'm trying."} BUT HE NOT TRY ENOUGH AND I SWIPE TO PUSH HIM AWAY AND HIT HIM TOO HARD AND HE FALL AND HE DEAD. I TRY TO EAT HIM BUT HE TASTE LIKE METAL SO I DO NOT EAT HIM. I DO NOT EAT.

Giant Has
Seething
Breakdown

I FIND VILLAGE. VILLAGE BIG WITH MANY HOUSE AND FARM AND SHOP AND CHURCH AND COBBLESTONE. TINY HUMAN SCREAM. I EAT HUMAN. I EAT SO MANY HUMAN. I WAIT FOR HUMAN TO REVENGE AGAINST ME BUT ALL THEY DO IS CRY. I ASK, "WHY DO YOU NOT REVENGE AGAINST ME?" AND THEY DON'T ANSWER THEY CRY SO I SAY, "I WILL EAT UNTIL I AM REVENGED AGAINST." SO I EAT OLD LADY. SHE TASTE LIKE SMOKE. I EAT DOG THAT TASTE LIKE CAT. I EAT CHILDREN SO EASY TO EAT CHILDREN NOTHING MATTER NOW. I EAT PRIEST. PRIEST TASTE SOUR LIKE LEMON TREE. I EAT NUN. I EAT ANOTHER NUN. NUN SCREAM AND SAY PRAYER AND I EAT NUN. I EAT ALL FARMER. FARMER TASTE LIKE DUNG. I EAT ALL COW AND ALL HORSE. I GO TIRED BUT STILL NO REVENGE. I TEAR HOUSE ROOF. I SET

FIRE TO HOUSE. I SMASH CHURCH. DAY IS DONE. DARK SO I DREAM.

After Meal,
Giant Dreams

I DREAM OF GIANT BIGGER THAN ME, BIG AS MOON WHEN ROUND AND RED. GIANT SAY, "I EAT YOU" AND HE EAT ME STARTING WITH STOMACH. WHEN HE OPEN MY STOMACH ALL PEOPLE FALL OUT, ALL CHILDREN LIVE AND ESCAPE AND I CRY I SO HAPPY! EVEN DUCK ESCAPE AND I DIE BUT SMILE AND HE EAT ME AND NOW THAT GIANT IS THE MOON AND THE MOON HAS MOUTH BIGGER THAN WORLD.

After Giant Dreams,
A Question

WE BORN TO BE EATEN, RIGHT? BUT
IF NO ONE BIG ENOUGH TO EAT YOU
THEN WHY YOU EVEN BORN?

Giant Waiting

I CRY OUT TO SKY. SCREAM TRAVEL FAR. I EAT BIRD IN SKY BY JUMPING. I BURN FOREST AROUND VILLAGE. I BURN THE BURNING VILLAGE. I PICK TEETH WITH BONE. I GATHER SKULLS AND MAKE SICK GRAVEYARD OF VILLAGE. I SMEAR BURNT HOUSE AND BURNT SHOP WITH POOP AND I PEE IN FLAME. I MASTURBATE EVERYWHERE AND SEED FALL ON DEAD GRASS LIKE STICKY HAIL. I SAY THAT I AM KING OF HATE. I VOMIT HUMAN GUT AND SMEAR HUMAN GUT ON CHURCH AND SAY, "NEW RELIGION IS WORSHIP RUIN." I SLEEP FOR MONTH.

Then

TODAY I WAKE FROM SLEEP AND YOU ARE THERE ON NOSE. YOU SMALL AND HOLD KNIFE TO MY EYE. YOU LOOK LIKE YOU FROM VILLAGE. LAST BOY SURVIVE. YOU HESITATE AND LET ME TELL STORY. BUT NOW YOU KNOW. I AM DESERVE DIE. WHY YOU HESITATE? YOU SO SMALL. BUT YOU MUST. PLEASE. KILL ME. TRY. YOU WILL BE BIG AS EARTH. TRY. EAT ME AND YOU WILL NO LONGER BE HUNGRY. TRY.

EVERYTHING
WILL BE
REALIGNED

EVERYTHING

EVERYTHING

WILL BE EVERYTH

WILL BE

REAL BE

EVERYTHING

WILL BE EVERYTHI

BE WILL BE

REALIGNED

WILL

EVERYTHING

WILL BE

REA WILL BE

1.

Everywhere I go there is construction and that is when I realize that it is the construction that is, in fact, everywhere. *Infrastructure realignment* reverberates in my head and the words drop from my mouth, falling on my nephew and the newly paved asphalt. He can't quite hear me, the bulldozers at each end of the street so inviting. He just nods and says, Yes, uncle.

We enter a café, and even the café, this tiny three-table six-chaired café, is being remodeled. A large, bearded man in blood-red flannel chops the wall to our right with an ax. Two small children remove the long front windows and begin hammering in wooden beams to take their place, and in between the wooden beams blades of sunlight slice the back of our heads and I coo, and I tell my nephew that everything needs realignment, I reassure him of this.

He nods. His eyes follow the tile floor. To reward him, I order a cherry scone. To reward myself I order a coffee but the coffee maker, the cashier tells me, is being improved, and these things take time.

2.

There are things my nephew and I do not talk about. We do not talk about his third-grade classes and his third-grade homework and his third-grade friends. I do not ask him if he's kept up with his Korean, like my sister said he would when she told me, *I don't want him to be like us.* I do not ask him why my sister no longer answers my calls or why she is absent when I visit. I do not ask him if his unemployed father really requires a babysitter or gets pleasure from rewarding me with this burden.

After we leave the café, my nephew and I, we breathe freshly baked tar. Our lungs become warm and lazy. A pipe is dislodged and bubbling mud water rushes below our feet, soaks right through my leather shoes. An ugly moistness squishes between my toes with every step I take, but I continue, unafraid.

We do not talk about the bruise under his right eye. We do not talk about the secret language crisscrossing my arms.

Instead, I point at the orange cones that fantastically line up — a giant V — across the block before us, leaving us only a shrinking sliver to traverse. We squeeze and twist our bodies over and around people who do the same. Some are wearing helmets in preparation for falling debris. Knee pads, boots, and gray steel mesh gloves. People living in constant terror. Somewhere, a building implodes, and the dust and smoke whips across our backs like a giant wave and he bristles, my nephew, at this rush of destruction. So I have to teach him that this is necessary. I grab him by his arms. I crouch to his eye level so he can learn my cross face. His eyes are like my eyes; I want to scream. I want to give him a bruise under his left eye so that there is symmetry. I tell him, Do not bristle. Things must be redone.

He nods, but he doesn't listen. No one listens anymore.

3.

They grab me by my arms and legs and dump me into a steel wheelbarrow. There are six men, identical. They have large raised cheekbones and deep black eyes and long white coats, but these men are not doctors. They are construction workers. They even have the yellow construction hats. As we pass the skeletons of buildings, bleeding wire and steel grating and plywood, the construction workers, they say: We must change you. "They tip the wheelbarrow in a garden of pink and violet asbestos, and I drop onto a rectangular slab. I shiver at the cold rock beneath my naked skin. Above me, dust has formed tiny spiral clouds. The men extend their measuring tape and rulers across my flat chest. They measure the distance between my nipples. They pinch the fat at my sides. They pull open my Korean eyes, as if I were hiding my pupils. (I was! I was!) They write fractions over my drooping stomach and across my sagging right arm — they use my scars as vincula to separate numerators and denominators (math is another secret language) — and I can't tell what the numbers are, but the men nod, and one of them, the one with a sledgehammer, he takes out my left leg below the knee. Before I can complain, someone twists on a new leg, inserting it over exposed bone, a jackhammer leg that rattles and spits. They saw off my callused hands with a timed motion, and one, and two, and three, and the hands slap the ground. My new right hand is a staple gun, the left a wrench that bites the air like a crab's claw, and can probably take off their heads, but these men do not care. They twist my head around and around, and my skull pops right off, and they spin on a new head, a handsome head. Gone are my hideous eyes and my yellow skin, my ugly buck teeth! If only my sister could see me now! This head is bleached white, has beautiful straight hair and dimples and youth. This head is aligned perfectly to who I am meant to be. I will tell my sister this, I think. And then I don't think anymore because my brain is a different brain and I am a different person. This was my dream.

4.

When I wake, I'm in need of a snack, but inside my kitchen my refrigerator is being sawed in two by technicians. They wear goggles and surgical masks. They do not regard me when I ask if I can take out the food first. They just press silver square buttons on their remotes and a long mechanical arm with a spinning saw sparks blue and gold against the door of my poor, obsolete refrigerator.

My sister calls me, finally. Why does my son have two black eyes? she asks.

Symmetry, I say.

What happened to you? she asks. She's crying.

Nothing, I say. Doesn't she understand? This is exactly the problem! I want to scream at the injustice. But then I realize that I'm just jealous of the refrigerator.

MY CALCULATED
VENGENCE
AGAINST
JOHN PHILLIP BATEAST
AND ALL
WHO LOVE HIM!

MY CALCULATED VENGENCE AGAINST

AGAINST JOHN PHILLIP BAT

N PHILLIP BATES MY CALCULATE

Y CALCULATED VENGENCE

AND ALL WHO LOVE HEM

ENGENCE AGAINST

HO LOVE HIM

AGAINST JOHN PHILLIP BATE

MY CALCULAT

PHILLIP BATES AND ALL

VENGENCE

JOHN PHILLIP BATES HIM

CALCULATED AGAINST

VENGENCE AND ALL

JOHN PHILLIP BAT

WHO LOVE MY CALCULA

AGAINST HIM

VENGENC

N PHILLIP BATES LOVE

51

I Capture and then Attempt to Recruit Claire de Raveneaux, Heiress to Unfathomable Wealth and Lover to the Lecherous John Philip Bateast!

I marched her down to her wine cellar with my machine gun aimed square against her quivering spine. I told her, "You will come to no harm. I am here to recruit you for a greater cause."

"How sublime!" she exclaimed. That evening, expecting to appear at an art gallery, she had donned a tight red dress that revealed flesh at: her back, her cleavage, her legs, her arms, just as he wanted her to. I would win her over as the first course of my vengeance against adventurer and fiend, John Philip Bateast!

I pointed my machine gun to a mahogany chair and when she paused, I pushed her onto it. "How gauche!" she remarked. But we were just getting started.

"I know that you feel as though you have found an important role by aligning yourself with the scoundrel and fiend, John Phillip Bateast. But you know the truth as much as I do. You know that you will be cast aside like all of the rest. Instead, you can make a new path and join me, as equals. Together, we will become the new adventurers of mystery and daring. With you by my side, I will finally have my revenge!"

All had gone according to plan. I had shot her guards, dismantled all the phones, drank most of the wine in her cellar, suffocated her golden retriever, flushed down her goldfish, poisoned her parakeet, decapitated her limo driver, and set fire to the limo. I destroyed everything she thought she needed to show her that she owned nothing in this world except herself.

After she joined with me, I would set fire to her mansion too, and her winter home, her beach house, her secret hideaway, and her ancestral landmarks. We would need none of that artifice in the new world that we would build. But then: a terrible derailment! She was shaking her head and refusing my hand!

"Do you not wish to set the world ablaze?"

She laughed. "You cannot become an adventurer of mystery and daring, like my beloved John Philip Bateast," she said. "Because you are like me. A woman."

The Math

247: Men murdered by hero/murderer John Phillip Bateast. (216 from "ethnic" countries.)

26: Books written on the exploits of John Philip Bateast.

30: Film adaptations produced in five countries. (USA, Bulgaria, United Kingdom, India, and France.)

536: John Philip Bateast fan clubs.

17: John Philip Bateast conventions a year.

23: Women murdered by henchmen in failed attempts at killing John Phillip Bateast.

1: Woman who desired vengeance.

At the Macy's Café, an Epiphany

I had been perusing the latest *Marie Claire*, lightly kissing each page with the soft of my index and ring fingers, scratching the perfume off an advert, tasting lavender on my nail, listening to the couple to the left of me love/bicker. Vanilla Spice Latte: I brushed lips against its whipped cream, licked cardamom, thought about the new beige linen curtains lording over the cottage desk at my bay window. And then I thought about whether I should spoon with Marcos or fellate Samuel or commiserate with Paul or sext Stephan, and such, and the like, and this was my life and I realized that I was *doing it again*.

55

Anonymous Women Who Have
Slept With John Philip Bateast Say:

"He doesn't so much love women as love skin. I saw him sucking on the inside of his arm when he thought I was asleep."

"He told me that he loved me and I knew he was lying. He told me that he needed me and I knew that he needed me and all women. We are the props."

"His penis is tremendous. It pains me to think that it will impale me again. Pains and *thrills me*."

"Do not ask me about John Philip Bateast! My heart cannot take more torture! It/I cannot endure!"

My Confrontation with the Cannibal King

We were in his studio apartment. I had broken in, in the dead of the night. He had been startled, but ready for me.

The Cannibal King had, many times, attempted to eat the heart of John Philip Bateast, believing that it would give him the vitality to live forever. John Philip Bateast had outfoxed and humiliated him at every turn. Here, with me, was his chance at redemption. Join me or perish.

I wanted him to say: "The root of my cannibalism stems from a repressed sexual desire to mate with my mother and annihilate my father/god. Because of the inevitable failure at that one sinister aim (that my entire existence hinges on), my body has constructed a hunger for the flesh of humans to subvert my diabolical intent. My constant desire for the heart of the deviant John Philip Bateast is a direct response to the failure that I know will forever shadow me. By failing against the vile John Philip Bateast, I am self-actualizing my repression and birthing my hidden nebulous failures into one that is concrete and quantifiable."

And I would have responded with, "How gauche!" But in secret, I would love him.

Instead he said, "All I am is hunger. Nothing else." So I killed him.

Story

Boy meets girl. Boy leaves girl. More on girl later. Boy wants more. Boy becomes pirate. Boy becomes captain of pirates. Boy is shipwrecked by tsunami. Boy fights cannibals on island. Boy leads cannibals to civilization. Boy betrays cannibals and becomes naval officer. Boy tours Bahamas. Boy is really secret agent. Boy makes love to many women. Boy is hero/murderer. Boy kills Somalians and Turks. Boy is called, by his enemies, the White Devil. Boy searches for secret Mayan gold. Boy finds secret Mayan gold underneath grave of King Janaab Pakal, loses Mayan gold, but finds self and then finds Mayan gold taken (by Mayans). Boy kills Mayans. Boy meets Chinese man and calls him Lotus Prince. Lotus Prince befriends boy and they journey to the Forbidden Kingdom. Treacherous Lotus Prince betrays boy in Forbidden Kingdom for thirty pieces of silver. Boy captures and imprisons Lotus Prince in Forbidden Kingdom. Boy saves and then makes love to many, many more women.

Girl sits in a Macy's café. Girl falls for cad or for rebel or for dark and mysterious man. Girl pines. Girl waits. Girl lingers. Girl wants to become.

Every story about a boy is Attack! Every story about a girl is Surrender!

Debate

Me: "And you are?"

Them: "We are loyal and faithful to John Philip Bateast, the lover, scoundrel, the international man of adventure and mystery, whose many journeys we have followed and who we will continue to glorify for he is blah blah blah —"

Me: *fires machine gun indiscriminately*

My Conversation with the Lotus Prince, Part One

He was imprisoned in the very center of the Forbidden Kingdom. A hut made of bamboo. They said that dragons guarded all prisoners there, but there were no dragons and no other guards, only the Lotus Prince, who sat on a straw mat, meditative.

The Lotus Prince had sharp yellow nails and a Fu Manchu beard, which made me groan. He was just like he had been written all of those years ago. He even wore that golden rubied robe that covered his delicate body.

I sat before him, and we drank green tea from bowls. I said to him, "I am committing vengeance against John Philip Bateast."

Said the Lotus Prince, "Confucius says, Vengeance is the path to blah blah blah."

"I have already met the Cannibal King. A disappointment."

"We are all the props in the adventures of John Philip Bateast."

"Not me."

"You were the very first prop." He sipped from the bowl. "I did not want to be a prop. I wanted to be the hero myself. I wanted to have a grand romance. I wanted to have flaws, but also virtues. But I don't even have a history. Not even a real name beyond the name that he gave me. I am just: Lotus Prince."

"Why could you not be more?" I said. "Because of John Philip Bateast?"

"Not him."

"I was one thing," I said, "but I am going to become something else."

"The only one that becomes is John Philip Bateast." He then stopped talking for a long while. The room emanated with his powerful silence, still and wise.

I asked, "Where are the guards? Why not escape?"

"We are all prisoners already."

"Of what?" I was tired of his riddles. Damn him!

He said, "How could you not know?"

Face to Face with
John Philip Bateast

We were on the roof of the Chrysler Building. He had chased me after I had shot at him in Central Park, while he was eating a scone with a new lover, and I had failed to fell him.

"Put that machine gun down, dear, or I will have to disarm you myself," said John Philip Bateast, who was debonair, calm, and handsome in his black tuxedo, even at these impossible heights.

"This is the final part of my vengeance," I said, trying to resist his charms. My machine gun wavered. I blamed the wind.

"I don't even know who you are, dear."

"I was the girl who was lost. The first. You were a boy. You left. You had adventures. All I did was want." I was hurt that he didn't remember. I didn't want the hurt but that's all I really had.

"I can tell that your flesh is glowing and delicious. How about instead of machine guns we have martinis at the Riviera, you beautiful creature?"

I was swooning with desire for him. *Something* was making me desire him! And that's when I realized that I was doing it again. I would always be doing it. I would never become.

My Conversation with the Lotus Prince, Part Two

"Why can't I become? Who is responsible for this? I will annihilate them!"

The Lotus Prince's eyes sparked with life for the very first time. His skin became pale. He was not himself (or he was more himself than ever). "Look, now! Turn around and see! They are always watching!"

That's when I saw you.

(TRANSLATED)

EXCERPTS FROM
THE KANAMITS'
TO COOK MAN
COOKBOOK

(TRANSLATED)
TRANSLATED EXCERPTS FRO
EXCERPTS FROM KANAMIT
CERPTS FROM
THE KANAMIT EXCERPTS FMA
KANAMIT
COOK
COOK TO
COOK BOOK TRANSLATED
OOK BOOK TRANSLATED BOOK
TRANS EXCERPTS FRO
TO EXCERPTS FRO
CERPTS FROM KANAMIT
E COOK THE KANAMIT MA
KANAMIT BOOK MA
TO COOK MA

A Braise of Man:

Brown man in oven for twenty minutes. Take out man and add a mirepoix of onions, carrots, and celery. Deglaze your pan with red wine. Add enough man blood (thinned with water) to saturate man, and then place man, covered in foil, back into the oven. Braise man in the oven at 300 degrees, until meat pulls away from the bone. Add lemon juice and parsley sprig for garnish. Success!

Serve Man with:

- Mashed potatoes
- Women (Diced)
- Mango

Humane Ways to Kill Man:

If you boil man alive, man will experience immense pain and will defecate in your bubbling water. To kill humanely, place man in the freezer for three days. Man will experience no pain as he slowly succumbs to the cold. His heart will just stop! Then you can remove man from your freezer and place man delicately into the boiling water. Also try: decapitation.

Vegetable Substitutes for Man:

*   Just kidding!

Testicle Tiramisu:

Preparing the biscuit layer is the most difficult part of Testicle Tiramisu. Make sure that the Savoiardi is soaked in espresso as well as Marsala wine. For the cheese layer, mix egg yolk, add sugar, and mascarpone. Beat egg whites until they form stiff peaks. Fold egg whites into the mascarpone/egg cream. Spread this onto the biscuit. Make sure the testicles are ground and moist. Sprinkle testicle bits onto the Tiramisu. You have completed your dessert offering! Congratulations!

Brain of Stephen Hawking:

This is the rarest of delicacies! When eating Brain of Stephen Hawking, use a hammer to crack the base of the skull. Remove, from the bone fragments, Brain of Stephen Hawking. Cut glorious Brain of Stephen Hawking with kitchen shears. Serve Brain of Stephen Hawking on flat-bread or water biscuit crackers for all your friends and guests.

To Eat Man Raw:

Not a pro in the kitchen? Eat man raw! Simply place man on table. As we all know, the easiest way to man's heart is through his ribs. But first, remember to tear off his skin! You should not eat the skin of man, which has fatty acids and excess grease. Place your fingers between the tiny bones within the rib cage. With a light tug the ribs will come off with ease! You can eat the heart of man. You can eat the liver. You can eat the spleen. You can eat the lungs. You can eat the stomach. You can eat the pancreas. You can eat the bladder. You can eat man's kidneys. If you eat the long intestine of man, you will also eat what he himself has eaten. You will eat his spaghetti. His kiwi. His ice cream sandwich. And then you will know man. Through his digestive tract you will know him. Truth: There is no better way to know anyone! Do not worry when you begin to have a feeling that tugs at your own heart and makes you weep. You're only realizing, at long last, that even you can be sated.

THANK GOD FOR FACEBOOK!

JUST WHEN WE DOUBTED HIS GOODNESS, MADELINE, THREE DAYS AFTER HER MURDER, UPDATED HER STATUS

THANK GOD FOR
MADELINE, THREE DAYS
FACEBOOK
AFTER HER MURDER
THANK GOD FOR
UPDATED HER STATUS
JUST WHEN WE
FACEBOOK!
GOODNESS
DOUBTED HIS GOODNESS,
JUST WHEN WE
THANK GOD FOR
THREE DAYS
MADELINE
HIS GOODNESS
DOUBTED
AFTER HER MURDER
AFTER HER MURDER
FACEBOOK!
MADELINE
UPDATED HER STATUS
UPDATED HER STATUS
AFTER HER MURDER
THANK GOD FOR
FACEBOOK
UPDATED HER STATUS
JUST WHEN WE
FACEBOOK!
HIS
GOODNESS
DOUBTED HIS GOODNESS
THANK GOD FOR
MADELINE, THREE DAYS
MADELINE, THREE DAYS
FACEBOOK!
AFTER HER MURDER
AFTER HER MURDER
UPDATED HER STATUS
UPDATED

"Thanks for the kind words!" she wrote.

We had posted all over her wall. How we missed her. How we knew she was in a better place. And she responded to our comments.

"miss u 2!!!"

"i AM in a better place fr"

"it's SO cool!"

"i know, im dead! wtf"

Shocked at first, we were then overcome with a sense of relief that our words were not in vain; that our comments actually held some importance; that there could be something connecting our world to the one beyond.

But we still had questions. I had questions. I'm her older brother; I'm supposed to have questions.

My first question was: "Who murdered you, sister?"

She answered, right on her Facebook wall: "the gym teacher DUH. he was like totally in love with me lol but his breath stank so i didnt go for it and he freaking killed me with a pipe!" It became clear why she hadn't responded to his comment on her wall —

the only one she had ignored. He had posted that they would honor her at the next basketball game. They would win it for her, he'd said.

We assaulted his Facebook page in response to her accusation, demanding that he turn himself in. "I AM INNOCENT," he posted on his wall, defiant, just hours later. We retaliated by defriending him, all of us, simultaneously. He responded by killing himself. Turned the engine on and closed up his garage. We wondered if he could get back on Facebook from where he'd likely gone. We waited for his friend request for weeks, months. He didn't friend us, which confirmed to us that though Facebook had reached Madeline, it wasn't accessible in hell. And there was justice in that.

My second question to Madeline was: "How did you get on Facebook from the other side?"

She answered, "God gives us 1 wish after we reach Heaven. some people wish to come back to life. some want to know all of the secrets of the universe. i wanted to get back on FB so I asked Him. i said, 'hey God, can you get me back on Facebook?' and then it was."

Seven hundred people liked her response.

This made sense to me. Madeline didn't have many friends while she was alive. People didn't pick on her;

they just didn't notice her. She only started getting attention on Facebook after she was killed and gained the popularity she'd never obtained when she was living. She had tried — she really had — but tried too hard, though. She paid attention to all the latest trends, buying the newest albums of the hottest pop stars. She went to the movies every Friday night so she'd be seen and have something to talk about on Monday. She stayed after school, joined groups she had no interest in like the student council or spirit club, because she thought it would raise her visibility. But it probably only raised scorn. Maybe if she hadn't stayed after school so much she wouldn't have caught the attention of the gym teacher, who was coaching the boy's football team and liked awkward, desperate girls, eager to please, trying to please. And maybe if I would've said something, told her she was perfect the way she was, maybe if I'd been a better brother, he wouldn't have had the chance to go after her, and she wouldn't have been killed. I wondered if she felt that way, but I didn't ask her. Other people had questions that took precedence. Many asked what God was like.

"oh He's cool," she said. "kind of a nerd, a cool nerd."

People responded with exclamation points, smiley faces.

"let me upload some pics," she said.

We almost died ourselves when she posted that.

But it took her two long weeks to put up the pictures.

During those two weeks people hounded her on her wall. "R the pictures up yet?" they asked with excited emoticons. "Can't wait to see HIM!" By the time two weeks had gone by, we wondered if she'd left us forever.

But Madeline finally came back: "sry 4 not posting! time doesn't work the same here! it's so weird lol"

She then posted the pictures. She made a whole album: GOD. She almost crashed the Internet. Almost immediately, her friends boomed from 900 to a million. God HIMSELF, right there for us to see. But here's the thing: He did look like a nerd. A guy with big square glasses, thin, with a short-sleeve, buttoned-up shirt and brown khakis. He smiled with Madeline as she took a picture of the two of them in an office building. Then in a parking lot. Then a video rental store.

The unspectacular nature of not just Him but His realm broke the enthusiasm over Madeline's return. Where were the clouds? The light? The glory?

Where was God?

Really? That's really HIM?

People couldn't help but post these comments,

especially when they saw the picture of God eating bruschetta and fried mozzarella sticks.

"someone wished for Buca di Beppo?" Madeline said, confused by our disgust.

"My God would not eat at a Buca di Beppo," posted Samantha, a deeply religious Mormon.

George Dundy, a guy Madeline had never even met, wrote bitterly, "What next? God at Macy's?"

"there isnt 1 in Heaven yet," Madeline replied. "but someone wished for a JC Penny last week and Gods putting in an order"

"Putting in an order? Fucking hell," George said. "Way to take the magic out of things." He was defriended the next day.

The rest of us didn't go as far as he did, but we felt the same disappointment. We stopped asking questions about the afterlife.

Madeline didn't get it.

Maybe she was just so caught up in the attention she had received. You score a million friends in one day and see what you do to hold on to them. Keep in mind, even though she was dead, she was still just a kid. Death doesn't bring wisdom, we learned, regretfully, from Madeline's posts and updates.

"SO BOOOOOOOORED," she declared one day. "I HATE FAKE PPL," she posted the next. And that wasn't the worst of it. She kept sending us applications for things like Mob Wars and Zombie Killers. She always responded to everyone's posts, all one million of us, since she had a whole afterlife to work with. On the worst days, she would post apologies and condolences for things that hadn't happened yet but that she knew about because chronological time has little meaning in Heaven. I learned my German shepherd, Rex, was going to die two days before it happened by way of her random comment: "Rex keeps licking my face lol" Emily Walters, Madeline's friend from high school, found out that her mother was going to die when Madeline posted: " cant believe what happened to yr mom! dont worry ill take care of her!"

She was becoming unbearable. People defriended her in droves. I tried to tell her that she needed to step back a little. But it was too late for me to be giving her advice.

In a last, desperate attempt to recapture our imaginations, Madeline began posting pictures of herself with dead celebrities like Marilyn Monroe, Elvis, even Benjamin Franklin. But they were doing things like high fiving, watching TV, and playing darts. As a community, we agreed it was in bad taste.

By the time those pictures went up, Madeline had lost most of her Facebook friends. She finished the rest of them off by posting: "it doesnt matter anyway the worlds ending in 10 years and all of u will have to deal w Judgment Day lol"

A low blow, to be sure.

But I stayed with her, despite the pressure. A part of me was glad that she lost all of her Facebook friends. I would finally have her all to myself.

I asked her how her day was.

She posted a sad face.

I posted: "I know and I'm sorry."

She posted: " it doesnt get easier even when yr dead."

"No, I guess not," I posted.

"i miss u," she posted.

"I miss you, too."

Smiley face.

Exclamation point.

Heart.

The Book

of the

London Green

THE BOOK OF THE BOOK OF THE BOOK LONDON GREEN THE BOOK OF THE BOOK LONDON GREEN THE BOOK OF LONDON GREEN THE BOOK BOOK THE BOOK OF THE THE THE BOOK OF LONDON GREEN LONDON GREEN THE BOOK

1. A History

We haven't seen the horizon since. We blamed the terrorists. The anarchists. Inevitably, the immigrants. But our fury did little to squelch the Green that hung above us, and us alone, a wave consuming the sky's blue in its soupy, impenetrable bubble like a declaration. A warning.

Of course, you know about the most radical changes already: The Thames evaporating into the Green, while the other rivers and streams remained untouched. The strange blue plants and then blue fungus that overgrew in our oldest wood and brick buildings, that proved calamitous for our most elderly, who breathed it in and later coughed it out in pools of purple blood until their throats became wretched and their bodies defeated. And the new smells emitting from this mass, a mix of soot and burning fat, a constant odor that is still hard to ignore, even to this day. And how could one not mention the children born, cursed, with the red eyes, dark like blood.

Understand that London has faced horrors before.

Our historians will tell you about the Great Smog of 1952, where pollutants in the air, mostly from coal, formed a thick layer of smog over the city for nearly a year. They will tell you about the miasma of the late 1800's, where the chimney smoke and mist from our long-departed Thames combined to devastate the city, in a fog that had a consistency of pea soup. After they remind you of that, your attention may return back to the Green above us, floating steadily, bubbling, calm. The historians will tell you that with proper air restrictions, and change of habits, the smog and the fog were beaten. And so will go the Green.

So we wait.

2. Trout

He was thirteen and wanted to see the sky beyond the Green. He wanted to see the Sun. His parents had been killed in the mass riots. Transport by boat and train was still possible, though the Green prevented entry by air, and this made leaving London scarce, valuable — for privileged few.

His old grandmother, coughing up purple blood on her deathbed, she grabbed him sullenly, and she stared into his dark red eyes, and she clutched onto his hands, and she clutched at her throat, and she died.

With her death, he felt that he had no reason to stay.

Now, Victor Trout was not a child born from love. Trout was born from need. Trout was born into struggle and only knew struggle. He still remembered his parents teaching him to steal food from the nearby Tesco, sneak sandwich packs and chocolates past the guard with a smile from his dimpled face. A distraction. Trout was alone, and he wanted to see the Sun. He had heard about it from his grandmother; she had shown him pictures of the beautiful yellow ball over a clear blue sky. Though he knew it was impossible, he wanted to grasp that yellow ball. He wanted to feel the hot yellow sneak between his fingers.

3. We Will Prevail

The red-eyed children, born strangely adapted to these new conditions, were cursed to stay under the Green. When transported outside of London, most, with a few exceptions, would catch sight of the Sun, and, within minutes, go blind. That was when we knew that the Green was something more than an ecological disaster. Its cruelty reeked of sentience. And that chilled us to the bone.

And still, we continued. The Queen, and then, after she passed, the King, remained in London. They reminded us of the old hardships and how the royal family held strong. The London Blitz. The terrorist attacks. The plagues.

We always prevailed. We had to believe we would prevail. All the while, we would never admit that we would look to the Green, and we would whisper: Tell us what to do. Tell us what we did wrong.

4. Trout Steadies Onward

He robbed a rich young boy leaving a Kensington school, took his clothing and identification papers. He tied up the poor rich boy — blonde, with pale skin and a thin frame — and dropped him into a giant trash bin. This would give Trout a few hours, if he was lucky. His hair was already cut to resemble an appropriately appropriate young boy. His smile was polished to shine properly when asked for proper identification. He wore stolen blue contacts.

When he reached the tube at Camden, the threshold seemed overwhelming. Thousands of people clogged the station. People trying to burst in, people trying to file out, people trying not to be trampled in the onslaught. He had heard stories of the riots that broke out when whole zones were shut down, the fires that consumed parts of the city trapped by isolation. He calmed himself outside, when he looked at the Green above. Every once in a while, the Green would hum with a strange, melancholy glow. Sometimes the Green would drip tiny green drops onto the city, and he wondered if it was something like tears. And if it was tears, if it came from something like sadness, or maybe, horrifically, something resembling love.

5. What We Did to the Immigrants

You know very well what we did to the immigrants.

6. Trout's Grandmother Speaks to Him on Her Deathbed, Before Succumbing

You live long as I have you see things that aren't worth seeing. The things that get ingrained. I wish I could choose what I remember. My baby girl at her best. Before all that poison she put in herself. After I worked doubles at the plant so she could get that dress. Seventeen but could have been thirty. Slim. Graceful. Confident. An actress or an ambassador. Loved that dress. Didn't want to take it off after prom. I wanted her to love me as much as that damn dress. Or love me more because of it. But that wasn't her way. So I want to remember that dress. That love. But for the life of me, I don't recall the fabric, or if it fell below her knees. All I know I know is the color. Golden yellow. Like from the Sun itself. Like if you touched the dress, you would sear your fingertips.

7. Trout Nearly Almost Makes It Through Safely

Just when he'd made it into the station, and he'd fooled the exhausted guards with his fool blue eyes, and he'd passed them the papers and so passed himself off as the rich boy, and his charming boy smile seemed to charm the elderly women who smiled, charmed, though still stared curiously at a smiling, charming boy, curiously alone — just when he thought he was going to make it, a news feed streaming by the pole to his left: A young boy found in a trash dumpster at Kensington, traumatized, real tears in real blue eyes, stripped naked and papers stolen. Papers which, in a short time, they'd trace back to the tube, back to where he was standing, waiting for the train to Brighton that was now stopping where he stood. That was when he ran from the train, sliding through police and crowds, and made his way onto the tracks and into darkness.

8. What We Would Have Told Trout

Understand: If we leave, we will be the first. We will be known as a generation of cowards. Traitors to our beloved city. Nothing better than the dirt devoured by worms.

Do you think we haven't dreamed of leaving?

Do you think we do not feel imprisoned?

You don't understand: This is more than what we want. If we abandon London, the Green will win.

If we did not believe that, we would not endure. So we believe.

You insult us with your devotion to abandonment.

You could ruin us all.

9. Trout On the Tracks

The descent down the tunnel was so long and dismal that Trout felt like he was losing parts of himself, which he was. His shoes began to break apart. The clothing he stole caught on formations of blue fungus, mutated and sharp and angry, growing from the wall against which he lay flat while the trains flew past, the small gusts of wind they created a relief in the sweltering heat that matted against his skin, and the blue fungus would tear at the clothing as he snuck by, and the clothing would fall from his body. Even his blue contacts fell into the darkness, rejecting him.

That was when he heard noises. Others. Laying against the walls. Waiting for the next train to pass. Eight of them. Naked. Covered in black dirt and grime. But Trout couldn't see all that. Only their red eyes, glowing hungry.

10. London is About Memory

Take Victor Trout, for instance. He was in the tunnels for days, crawling through pathways long abandoned. With the other children. They were naked, ugly. He found it remarkable to find so many in worse conditions than him. One night he spent cradling a baby girl, a daughter of a girl not much older than himself, crying in the sweltering darkness of the tube's tunnels. He whispered a lullaby to the baby, trying to calm her. This lullaby was sung to him by his grandmother when he asked about the Sun. She would kiss him on the cheeks and lift him above her face, and she would cradle him as he was cradling the baby. The lullaby went:

Day is done, gone the sun
From the lakes, from the hills, from the sky
All is well, safely rest;
God is nigh.

When the others heard him sing this and saw the tears that came from the young boy, they used that as their mantra as they made their way through the black. Trout led them. He loved them, he realized.

And do you know what happened when they entered the light? When they saw the blue sky and the strange yellow ball? When the Green was just a memory in the distance? Trout held his hands out, and he reached for the Sun. He waited, with the others, to see if their eyes would flicker and fail. And he tried to loop the Sun in his finger, and fall into the blue, his eyes breathing it all in, a new, perhaps final, vision, and he kept telling himself, in a frenzy of ecstasy: Remember Forever Remember Forever Remember Forever —

I WILL TEACH YOU RETRIBUTION

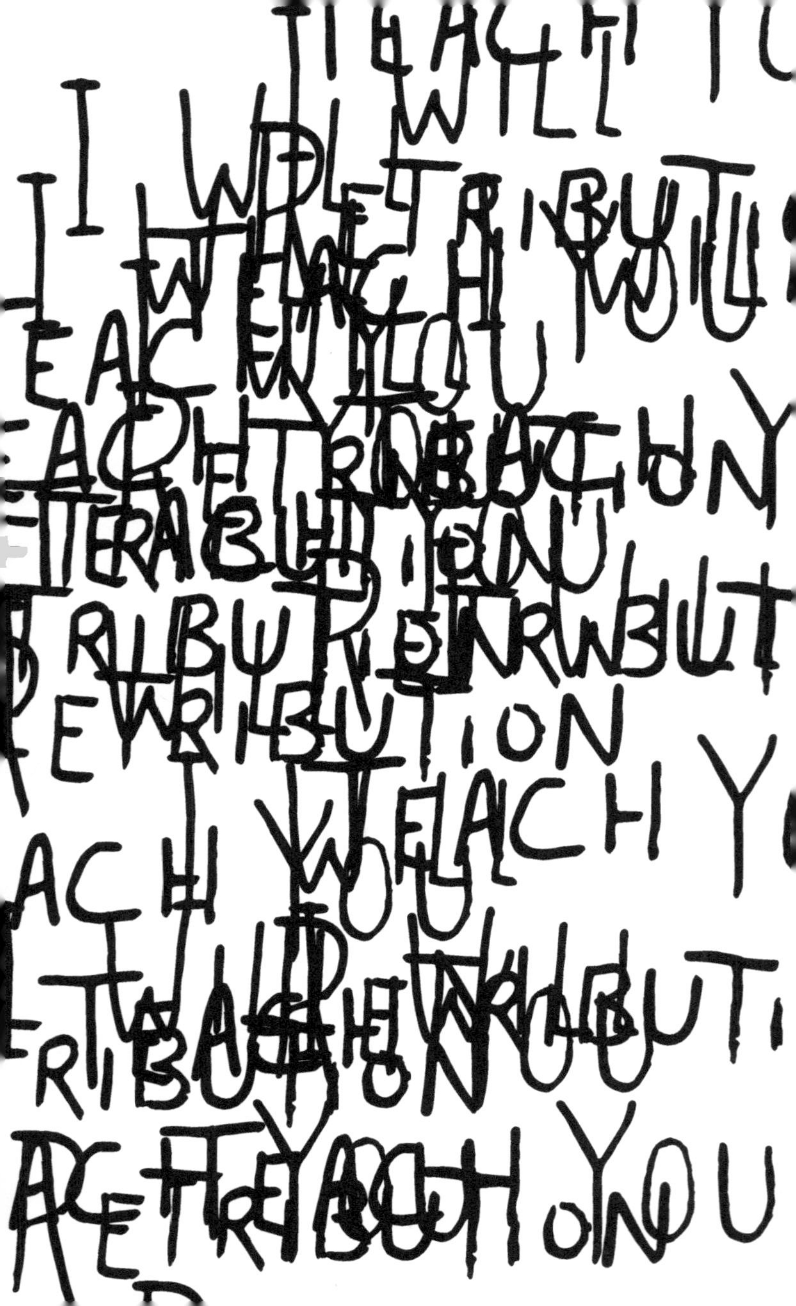

I WILL

RETRIBUTION

TEACH YOU

RETRIBUTION

TEACH YOU

Just when I thought I was finally rid of my husband, his spectral form returned and led to extreme agitation. When I turned on my Sanyo television set to fall deep into my fables, his gaping maw, his square chin, his very cheeks shaped like puffed lumps jutting from his face, a grotesque sight that had convinced me on that night three weeks before to splay the acid across his face — this face! — it was there before me, inside my Sanyo television set, undisturbed.

"Leave my Sanyo television set at once," I of course said, hands inching towards the vial of acid I had saved for just such a happening, for fear of his returning.

"You shall not splay acid upon my high-definition maw," he said, his voice booming through the high-definition Toshiba speakers hanging from the ceiling. "You shall not cause harm to fall on your beloved Sanyo television set and high-definition Toshiba speakers. This I know," he boomed.

It was as if the other side had imparted him with a wisdom unseen in his living life! For he knew that I would certainly not inflict harm on my beloved Sanyo television set, the magnificent, high-definition plasma behemoth, hanging gracefully against the pristine drywall walls. I would rather bring harm against my right hand!

"You have taken my life," he said, "by splaying acid upon my face and upon my eyes. Prepare to experience your retribution."

As if he knew a thing about retribution! A frigid, childless marriage — this is the ultimate retribution, and I had paid it in multitudes immeasurable, as punishment for a crime I had not yet (but was always destined to!) commit. But I did not tell him this, then, the words escaping me in my fit of high emotion. I was tempted to shut the Sanyo television set off, but my favorite fable, *Sunny Side Park* was on. We saw its main characters — Desi, Monica, and Charles — trapped in a burning hotel room, with a decision to be made on whose life Monica would save:, her current lover, Charles; or that of the man who she lusted over: Desi, a wild Spaniard of a man who I also lusted over, who America, too, lusted over, who the world itself lusted over, under, after.

So, I watched. Enthralled by the ensuing drama, my husband propped himself in a corner of the screen, and he watched too.

***

After two weeks of this continuing melodrama I decided that it was enough, that he would certainly have to go! The last straw came when Desi left the room in the hotel, in an act of defiance and self-sacrifice, and he, my husband, said, "Desi is a fool to do this; he will burn."

And I said, "The only thing he cares about is the burning within his heart."

"The only thing he should be concerned with is the burning upon his flesh. I know of the conditions in which flesh can withstand bodily harm, from when you splayed the acid upon my maw, and when the acid ate away at the skin down into my bone," said my husband. "All that matters is the flesh."

"And what of the passion burning within the heart," I said.

And he did not answer, for he knew nothing of the passion, not in his living and now his dead life.

It was then that I knew that I had to rid him a second time, and this time I would need help, to sever him from the Sanyo television set that I so adored.

***

This is where I say hello to the Triplets, who couldn't be older than ten, the three of them, these three identical boys with their yellow bowl-cut hair, identical in their three-piece gray suits with suit shorts and long socks, six eyes the same bluish green like the sea during early summer days.

I did not expect children to come when I answered the advertisement regarding my poltergeist predicament that had caused me manic episodes and unceasing worry. In the paper they did not say their ages. The paper simply read: *We will rid you of meddling poltergeists from any object they may occupy.* The Triplets, it read, *will be of service to you in such a manner of complete satisfaction.*

But there were the boys, standing, emotionless, waiting for me to let them in.

"Boys?" I said. "I did not expect boys to face the poltergeist that has taken ahold of my Sanyo television set."

"We are boys," the middle one said, for they were standing side by side, shoulders touching, backs straight. "When we were younger children, a demon shaped like the Moon entered our small home and slaughtered our parents, devouring them. We saw into the hellfire eyes of the beast and were forever changed, tasked to track down the hounds of hell with help from a vision and the touch of the other side, and we will bring retribution upon those who would cause any harm onto the living, now that we are older children. Please let us in. It is raining."

In my blazing fall into the abyss I had not noticed that it was pouring, and their straight locks of hair were being dampened by the wet tears of the sky! And they did not even shift under the weight of the water, these poor boys, how I wanted to grab them then and hold them close against my breasts!

I hastily brought them inside and gave them towels to wrap around their bodies and set fire to the fireplace and ushered them to sit in front of it, and I even brought a pillow for them to sit on, and they remained still, against the red and yellow flames.

"We will start soon," said the middle boy, who I named Leader, since he seemed to speak for them all. "Where is the apparition?"

"The apparition is inside of my Sanyo television set and will not come out," I told them, passing them mugs of cocoa with marshmallows drowning inside, their bottoms bobbing on the surface.

Leader said, "Inside of your Sanyo television set. We see. We will deliver unto him retribution after we drink our cocoa with marshmallows."

***

The Triplets paced around the living room, removing the wires connecting the Sanyo television set to the high-definition Toshiba speakers. This operation unnerved me. "Did I hire electricians or exorcists?" I asked, alarmed that they would bring unwarranted changes to my home theater apparatus.

"We are not exorcists," one of them said, not Leader this time. His voice was higher, shrill. If these were my children and I had raised them and fed them from my breasts, this one would not be my favorite. I called him Annoying.

"Must you disconnect the high-definition Toshiba speakers from my Sanyo television set?"

"We must," said the third one, who I had not heard before. His voice was plain, sadder than the others. As if he had witnessed more of the horrors then his brothers had and was at some loss because of it. I called him Sad.

And what of Leader? He sat, meditating, his eyes underneath his lids, penetrating the other side, or maybe the other side of that.

"Please turn on the Sanyo television set," he said, after a long silence.

I turned it on. "Beware," I warned them. "He will lie to you. He will torment you."

My husband shook his high-definition head. Behind him was a game show with a spinning wheel whose half-hour of spinning we both suffered so that we might get to *Sunny Side Park* without fear of missing a thing.

"Is this the demon?" Leader asked.

"I am not a demon," said my husband. His voice was softer, the high-definition Toshiba speakers disconnected, leaving his voice hollow and small, coming from the Sanyo television set that, though having a beautiful frame and picture, lacked the dimensions of adequate sound and had forced us to purchase the high-definition Toshiba speakers in the first place.

"The demon!" I screamed.

My husband breathed in deeply and then sighed. "I want to watch *Sunny Side Park*. At least give me one more episode of *Sunny Side Park*."

I considered this. We had followed their death-defying cross against the flames of the hotel, and this episode promised to provide us with a choice, finally, for Monica to make in a suitor. *Sunny Side Park* was truly the only thing we had ever shared.

"Please," he said.

"We will start the process of your disentanglement," said Leader. "This will take time. You will have time to see this episode of your program."

My husband nodded. "There will be a choice this episode."

"There is always a choice," said Leader. And they proceeded to outline the floor with white chalk, encircling their little boy bodies.

***

My husband had always refused to give me the gift of a child. In our lovemaking I had begged him, I had said, "Make me warm inside with your liquids and with the thousand swimming yous, and let them reach the tree of life, the pumping egg which yearns for your seed."

And he refused, and he always came onto my stomach, the disagreeable warm goo slapping against my bellybutton, smearing the skin, sitting above the core of my burning being, the home for a child I would never have.

If we would have had children when we were warranted to have children, they would have been the age of the Triplets who were pressing black chalk against my drywall walls, inscribing hieroglyphs, crows and bats and three-headed dogs, to an incredible and detailed degree, to their finest hairs, as my husband watched the ends of the game spinning show.

Maybe that is why I had made them chicken noodle soup and turkey sandwiches and presented them as a mother craving their absolute love and affection. And maybe that is why I said to them, "You will have the food if you kiss me upon my cheek, and whisper in my ear the one gift that you would cherish above all others."

Their hands matted with chalk, they obliged: Leader first (of course!), kissing me on the cheek tenderly, my breasts swelling with the desire to feed them, to nourish them. "I want a video game console," he whispered in my ear. And I answered, within myself, Yes, yes, I will give you this for your love!

Annoying came next, kissing me roughly, and whispered, piercingly, "I want a toy gun." And I said, inside the cellars of my heart, Yes, this can be so.

Sad came last, begrudgingly, barely touching my cheek with his lips. And I didn't even feel the warmth of his breath when he said, "I want my parents back."

***

Monica chose Desi.

Both of them were on either side of the doorway, beckoning her to come with them for survival. Their usual dapper appearances were marked with desperation and black smudges from smoke inhalation, smearing across their faces in systematic variations.

True love was victorious! I beamed. As Monica took Desi's hands, and Charles could only watch as the two of them made it through to the elevator shaft to possible death, fiery insatiable passion included, as the screen marked: To Be Continued.

My husband was not pleased.

"Their flesh will melt," he said. "She chose wrong

and now all the three of them will perish.”

"It is time," Leader said. He had a scythe in his right hand and a body a little larger than himself made of straw in his left, an accurate drawing of my husband thoughtfully placed where a face would be. I could barely contain my giggling, to be finally rid of my husband who had caused me such unimaginable sorrow!

Annoying held a book of incantations and started humming in a Gaelic tongue, the words cutting against the roof of this mouth. I could not understand why they had chosen him for this task, his voice causing so much irritation in the space between my ears. Or maybe that was the reason he was chosen, the pain he would cause being that much more efficient in driving the demons out.

Sad tearfully touched the screen, staring into my husband's eyes.

"This will hurt," he told my husband.

"Whatever," my husband answered, recalling, I'm sure, Monica's jump into Desi's arms. "It doesn't even matter anymore."

***

After the retribution, I took the Triplets out to the ice cream shop and we had ice cream cones, piled three scoops high: strawberry, chocolate, and pecan.

"We thank you for the ice cream and the turkey sandwiches and the chicken noodle soup," said Leader.

I smiled.

We were at a table outside. The air was cool, the smell of rain drying from the Earth and the day melting into night.

They could be mistaken for my own children, except for that I had dark brown hair, and not the yellow locks that covered their heads. I wanted to lap their heads with my tongue, like a mother cat cleaning her kittens after trudging through a garden of mud.

But I didn't tell them that.

I said, "I want to take you three and make you my children."

They nodded, understanding. "We understand," said Leader. "But you can only take one of us."

Only one of them! It was like choosing which leg to dismember!

Leader was unmistakably my favorite, but the choice was not so simple, for I feared that he would outgrow me quicker, and, upon entering adulthood, grow tired of me, ignoring my letters and calls. Truthfully, I thought he was too good for me. Unwanted was Annoying, unless we could make some agreement where he would not be allowed to speak in my presence, something that could be difficult to arrange in the circumstance where he was in danger, or in need of milk.

So, my greedy eyes came upon Sad. Oh, what I would do to fill him up with cheer! I would stuff him within a book bag and carry him in front of me, like a kangaroo would its joey. And he would suckle on my breast from this pouch, and the pouch would lie against my naked skin, and we would be only two layers — pass the flesh and meat — from bone, and one more layer from my beating, beautiful heart, and that would be the only distance between us, those fine layers, and we would skip into the horizon, and our hearts would burn.

THE WRITER EXITS DRAMATICALLY

THE WRITER EXITS
WRITE THE WRITE

Them: "We'll stop you!"
Me: "You'll try!"

slides into open car door, drives away

***

Them: "Are you a Barnes and Noble member?"
Me: "I hold no allegiances."

jumps into boat, sails away

***

Them: "Excuse me, sir, do you have the time?"
Me: "Time is an illusion."

runs into train, grabs a seat, waits a minute and then the train departs

***

Them: "Who do you think you are?"
Me: "Who do you got?"

grabs cowboy's horse, hops onto the saddle, and rides into the sunset

***

Them: "I worked a double yesterday. I'm so tired!"
Me: "Sleep when you're dead."

commandeers dirigible, plunges it into the Atlantic

***

Them: "Where are you going?"
Me: "I have to find something."
Them: "What?"
Me: "Myself."

jumps out of spaceship, spaceship explodes behind

***

Them: "Believe in your dreams."
Me: "No. Believe in yourself."

*tears hole in fabric of space, jumps into parallel dimension,
is never seen again*

Acknowledgments

The stories in this collection have been previously published, in slightly different form, in *McSweeney's Internet Tendency*, *Ghost Ocean Magazine*, *Thieves Jargon*, and the *Chicago Reader*. Much appreciation must be given to Long Day Press and their tireless work. Additional thanks go to the students and faculty at Roosevelt University who have read my work and have given me valuable feedback, and the wonderful people at Kundiman, with special thanks to my friends in the Third Dessert. I must also thank booksellers everywhere — you are truly the salt of the Earth, and the pepper too. Special thanks to Martin Seay for his thoughtful blurb (everyone who hasn't should read his book, *The Mirror Thief*, NOW). Additional thanks (and apologies) go to my sister and my parents. And, of course, thank you to my wife, and the love of my life, Ellen.

Timothy Moore is a Korean American writer and instructor living outside Chicago. He has work published in *McSweeney's, Midnight Breakfast, Ghost Ocean Magazine,* and the *Chicago Reader,* among others. He is a Kundiman and Luminarts Fellow, and has had a Hinge Arts Residency. He has worked at a number of independent bookstores and universities and has his MFA in Creative Writing from Roosevelt University.

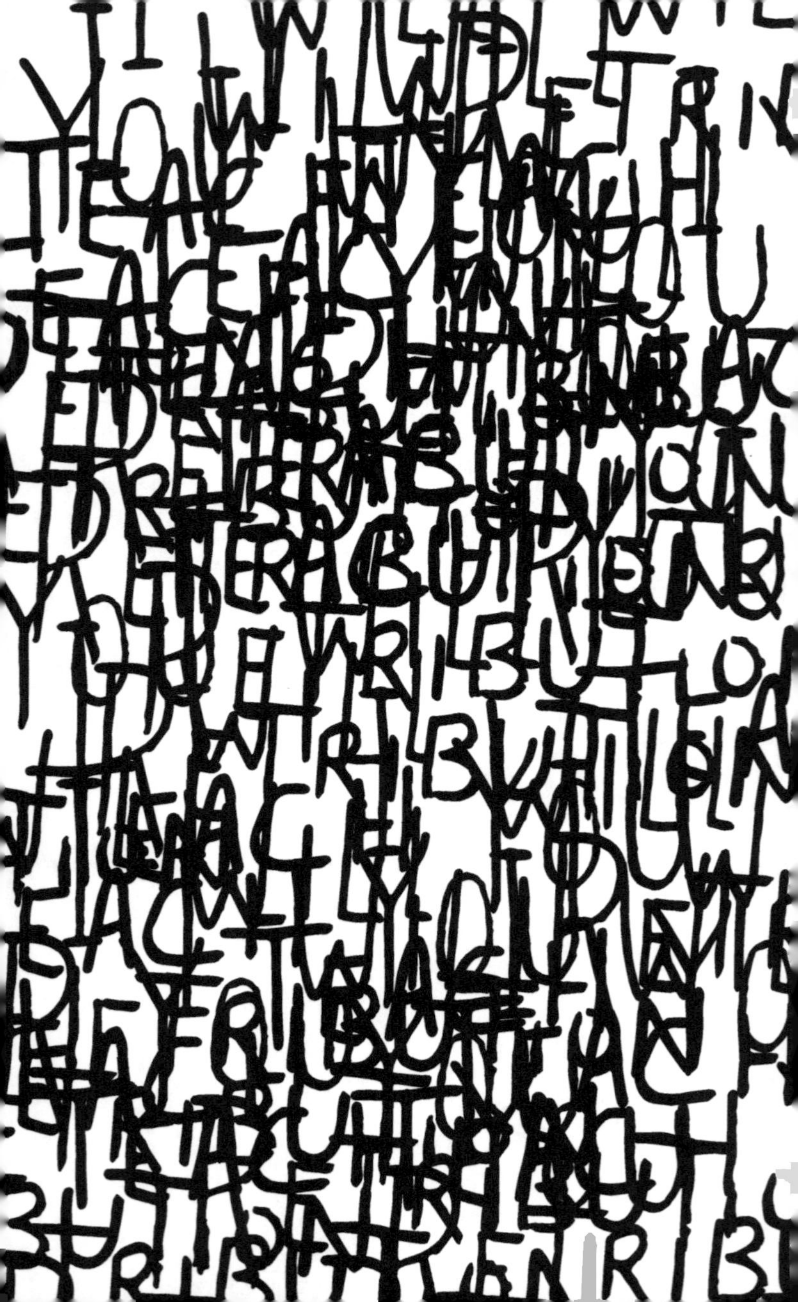